To Allan and family – A.J.

Text copyright © Ann Jungman 2002
Illustrations copyright © Chris Molan 2002
Book copyright © Hodder Wayland 2002

Consultant: Jonathan Gorsky, The Council for Christians and Jews
Editor: Katie Orchard

Published in Great Britain in 2002
by Hodder Wayland, an imprint of
Hodder Children's Books

Cataloguing in Publication Data
Jungman, Ann
Waiting for Elijah.: a story about Passover. –
(Celebration stories)
1. Passover – Juvenile fiction
2. Children's stories
I. Title
823.9'14 [J]

ISBN: 0 7502 3651 5

Printed in Hong Kong by Wing King Tong

Hodder Children's Books
A division of Hodder Headline Limited
338 Euston Road, London NW1 3BH

CELEBRATION STORIES

Waiting for
Elijah

Ann Jungman

Illustrated by Chris Molan

HODDER
Wayland

an imprint of Hodder Children's Books

Passover is a very happy time in the Jewish calendar, because it is a double rejoicing. Both the sweetness of freedom from slavery and the arrival of spring are being celebrated as this festival takes place in March or April each year.

Passover is named after the time when the Angel of Death flew over Egypt, killing the first-born males in every house, but 'passed over' the Jewish houses and spared the Jewish children. The Jews were slaves in Egypt and were cruelly treated by Pharaoh and his servants. God decided that the Jews had suffered greatly and should be allowed to follow Moses into the promised land of Israel. After the death of the Egyptian first-born males, the Jews were allowed to leave. While the freedom of the Jews was precious, it was also accompanied by great suffering for the Egyptians.

A special ceremony called the Seder is held to remember this time.

The Seder takes place after dusk on the first night of Passover. The whole family gathers and there is a huge meal. Any strangers who have nowhere to go are also invited to the meal.

A Seder is made up of three parts. First of all the story of the Exodus from Egypt is told – everyone reads in turn from a book called the *Hagadah*, which tells the story. The children are encouraged to join in and the youngest asks questions of the older people about the traditions. Then the meal is eaten, and much of the food has a special meaning. The last part is the singing of traditional songs.

Every family lays a place for the Prophet Elijah in case he wants to come, and someone opens the door to invite the Prophet in. Jewish people believe that the Prophet will only come when the world is ready to be a better place.

"Why is this night different from all other nights?" Debbie said to her mirror. She smiled at her reflection. "Because it's a holiday and it's Passover, my favourite time of year," she answered herself.

"Debbie, what are you doing?" came her mum's voice.

"I'm just practising the four questions for tonight," shouted Debbie.

"Ah, yes," said Debbie's mum. "Could you come down? Gran and I have something to tell you."

Debbie bounced downstairs. As always on the day of Passover the house was full of lovely food smells – waves of cinnamon, almonds and herbs wafted towards her. Debbie burst into the kitchen.

"Mmm, I love the smell of Passover, Mum," she said. "What did you want to tell me?"

"Darling, I know you're going to be disappointed – but Uncle Danny is bringing young Ben to the Seder tonight," her mum said.

"That's great," smiled Debbie. She liked Ben.

"It means that you won't be the youngest at the Seder any more," said her mum gently. "So you won't be the one to ask the questions."

Debbie stared at her mum in disbelief. For as long as she could remember she had been the one to ask the questions.
Passover would not be Passover without that. The singing of songs was great, the food was delicious, seeing all the family and using the best silver and china was splendid. The  story of the escape of the Jews from slavery in Egypt was exciting, and finding the hidden matzah wafer was fun. But the best bit, the very best bit, was asking the questions. Tears rose in Debbie's eyes.

"But that's *my* job!" she shouted. "I do it every year. Ben's too young – he won't do it properly!"

"Sorry, Debs," said her mum. "The custom is that it's always the youngest person who asks the questions."

"That's a silly custom," moaned Debbie. "It's time it was changed."

Debbie's mum tried to calm her down. "You can have another job," she said. "You can be the one to answer the door to the Prophet Elijah."

But Debbie was not impressed. "I don't want to do that!" grumbled Debbie. "He never comes anyway."

"No more complaining, my darling," said her gran crisply. "Come on, I need your help chopping the apples and almonds. You help me every year, I can't do it alone."

"Later, Gran, OK? I'm too upset. Sorry!" And Debbie ran outside.

Bitter Herbs

Debbie ran to the end of the front garden, and out into the square. She sat down on a bench, and tried not to cry.

"It's not fair! It won't feel like a proper Seder if I don't ask the questions," she sniffed, as the tears began to run down her cheeks.

"Excuse me, young lady. Would you mind very much if I sat down on your bench?" came a deep voice.

Debbie looked up. A very old man with a long white beard, a black hat, and the bluest eyes Debbie had ever seen, stood smiling down at her.

"No, I don't mind," she said, and even managed a little smile. "You're a friend of our neighbours, the Steins, aren't you?"

"Yes, I am," replied the old man, raising his hat to her. "I'm staying with them for a while." And he slowly lowered himself down beside her, leaning on his stick.

"You look very sad," he continued. "Is there a problem in such a young life?"

"I'm not young enough, that's the problem,"
Debbie sighed. "It's the Seder tonight and I
always ask the four questions. But now my little
cousin, Ben, is going to do it instead."

The old man nodded. "When I was a boy, on
Seder night, I always used to ask the questions –
until one year my brother, Ephraim, had learned
to talk – and then it was his turn."

"Did you mind?" asked Debbie.

"Oh, yes, at first I was angry. It felt sour, like the bitter herbs we eat at the Seder."

"And then?" demanded Debbie.

"I got another job! I opened the door to the Prophet Elijah," he replied. "My name is Elijah, so that felt right to me."

Debbie giggled. "So Elijah opened the door to Elijah?"

"That's right," the old man replied.

"And did he come?" asked Debbie.

"Of course not! Elijah will only come when the world is ready to be a better place, and to welcome the Messiah. But one wonderful day he might come and we should be ready to let him in."

So opening the door to Elijah was really quite an important job. Debbie began to cheer up. She might enjoy this Seder, after all…

"You're just like Elijah!" she laughed. "Like
a wise prophet."

"Nonsense, young lady. I'm just Elijah
Myrovitz, born in Poland a long time ago, and
now living in America."

Debbie remembered that at Passover it was
important to be nice to strangers, because long
ago in Egypt the Jews themselves had been
strangers in a strange land. Elijah seemed to
be a long way from home, too.

Debbie had an idea. "Why don't you come to our Seder?" she asked. "I'd love you to come, and Mum wouldn't mind. We always invite anyone who is far from home."

The old man smiled.

"We don't live far away," encouraged Debbie. "In that house over there – the one with the bright red door. The Steins will tell you."

"I'll try," he promised. "Maybe not for the whole evening, but for a little while."

Debbie was delighted. Now she would be able to open the door to her own Elijah. She had her very own surprise Seder guest. Suddenly, it didn't matter that she wouldn't be asking the four questions any more.

"I must go back and help Mum and Gran with the cooking," she said. "They're buried under a mountain of food! See you tonight, Elijah – and thank you."

Sweet Things

Debbie raced back through the square and the front garden, and burst into the kitchen.

"You look more cheerful!" smiled Gran.

"Sorry I was so grumpy earlier," said Debbie. "I was really upset, but I feel much better now. I just met Elijah – and he says he's coming to our Seder!"

Debbie's mum and Gran caught each other's eye and smiled.

"That's wonderful, dear," said Gran.

"Yes, it *was* wonderful," agreed Debbie seriously.

Debbie's mum looked a bit worried. "You do know that Elijah is an *idea*, Debbie, not a *real* person," she said. "You won't be too disappointed when he doesn't arrive, will you?"

"It's OK, Mum. My Elijah *is* a person, and he *is* coming. And I've come back to help."

"Great," smiled her mum, doubtfully. "Now, let's see, where's my list? Ah, yes, the charoset. You'll need…"

Debbie finished her mum's sentence for her. "…Apples, cinnamon and almonds mixed with wine. Something sweet to remind us of the sweetness of freedom, after slavery."

"That's right," nodded Gran. "And can you remember the other reason why we make the charoset paste?"

Debbie frowned, trying to remember. "Something about the pyramids…"

"You're getting warm," said her mum, helpfully.

"I know! It's like the cement the Hebrew slaves used when they built the pyramids for Pharaoh!"

"Well done!" said Mum and Gran together.

"And then Moses came, and led his people out of slavery and into the Promised Land," said Debbie.

"Exactly," said Mum. "And when you've finished with the charoset, Debbie, you can put the matzot on the table."

Debbie pulled a face. "I don't like matzot," she moaned.

"Well we have to eat them at Passover – and I bet you can't remember why."

"Yes, I can," said Debbie. "To remind us that we had to leave Egypt so fast, there was no time for the yeast in the bread dough to rise, so we had to have flat bread without yeast."

"Quite right," said Debbie's mum. "Now go and put three matzot by your father's place and cover them with a cloth."

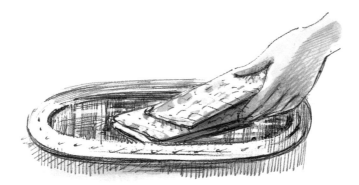

The Ten Plagues

That night, ten people were seated round
the table.

"You did lay an extra place for Elijah, didn't
you?" Debbie reminded her mum.

"I laid two – one for the Prophet, and one for
your friend," she replied, smiling at Gran.

Debbie's dad said the blessing and broke the
crisp matzot in front of him. Then he wrapped
one piece in a cloth and passed it to his wife.

Ben leaned over and whispered to Debbie, "What's he doing?"

"It's the afikoman," she told him. "We have to find it later."

And they saw Debbie's mum slip out of the room with the cloth-wrapped matzah.

Then it was time for Ben to ask the four questions. Debbie watched him, proud that he was doing a good job. *And it's fine that he's doing it,* she thought, *because I've got a truly terrific surprise for them all.*

"How is this night different from all other nights?" began Ben.

Debbie's dad answered, "On this night we eat only matzot, unleavened bread."

"How is this night different from all other nights?"

"On this night we dip the herbs twice," answered Debbie's dad.

Debbie encouraged Ben to ask again.

"How is this night different from all other nights?" said Ben, looking at Debbie to make sure he was doing it properly.

"On this night we eat only bitter herbs to remind us of slavery."

Ben grinned and asked the question one last time.

"On this night," said Debbie's dad, "we recline rather than sit."

"That means we can put our elbows on the table," Debbie whispered to Ben. "It shows that we are free people, not slaves. Slaves have to eat sitting on the floor."

Ben nodded.

Debbie's dad continued, "And the Lord heard our voice in bondage in Egypt and told Pharaoh, 'Let my people go,' but Pharaoh refused. So God sent ten plagues to make Pharoah change his mind."

Then he turned to Ben and explained, "Now I am going to read out the plagues. After each one you must dip your finger into your wine and flick it on to your plate."

Ben looked at him hard. He and Debbie both had their fingers ready over their glasses of wine.

There were plagues of blood, frogs, lice, vermin, cattle sickness, boils, hail, locusts and darkness.

And after each terrible plague, Debbie and Ben splashed some wine on to their plates.

Debbie's mum took up the story. "And even then, Pharaoh wouldn't let the Hebrews go. So God was very angry, and He sent the Angel of Death to fly over the houses of the Egyptians and kill the first-born boy in every house. He told the Jews to put a sign on their door posts, so that the Angel would 'pass over' their houses and not kill their eldest sons."

Solemnly, everyone at the table splashed the final drop of wine on to their plates.

"Did Pharaoh let the Jews go after that?" asked Ben.

"Oh, yes," replied Debbie's dad. "You see, the angel killed Pharaoh's eldest son, too, so he was very sad. Now, Debbie, you read for a bit."

Debbie picked up the *Hagadah*, which told the
story, and read it out. "As soon as the slaves had
gone Pharaoh changed his mind, and sent his
soldiers to bring them back. When the slaves got
to the Red Sea the waves parted in front of them,
and they walked through. Pharaoh's troops
followed in their war chariots, but the waves
closed over them and Pharaoh's army drowned."

"Every single one?" asked Ben, his eyes wide with amazement.

"So the story goes," nodded Uncle Danny.

Ben dabbed his fingers back in the wine. "Why can't we suck our fingers, Debs?" he whispered. "I want to know what the wine tastes like."

"I don't know," replied Debbie. "We can ask Elijah when he comes – *if* he comes, that is."

Elijah's Visit

The time crept round to nine o'clock. Debbie was beginning to give up hope of her Elijah turning up.

"He isn't coming," she sighed.

But then, just as everyone had finished eating, the doorbell rang.

"It's Elijah!" shrieked Debbie, jumping off her chair and racing to the door, "It's my Elijah!" She flung open the door, and there he was.

"You *did* come," laughed Debbie. "Oh, thank you so much!"

"It's a pleasure," he said. "Now, little lady, are you going to invite an old man inside?"

"Of course!" said Debbie.

She took Elijah by the hand and led him into the dining room. "This is Elijah," she announced proudly. "And he has come to our Seder, after all."

"Elijah Myrovitz," said the old man, smiling around the room. "I do hope I'm not intruding."

"You're very welcome," said Debbie's mum, laughing. "We thought that Debbie was making up a story about meeting Elijah. Happily, we were wrong – we're pleased you could come."

Debbie's dad invited him to join them at the table and the old man sat down.

"Have you eaten?" asked Debbie's mum. "There's still plenty of food."

"Oh, no, I ate with the Steins earlier. But a small glass of wine would be most pleasant."

"We were about to start singing, Elijah," said Dad, "I hope you enjoy singing."

"I love it," he replied.

Debbie touched his elbow and pulled him to one side.

"Elijah, can I ask you something first?" she asked quietly. "Why don't we drink the wine when we recite the Ten Plagues of Egypt?"

The old man sat back in his chair and rubbed his chin thoughtfully. "Ah, that's a good question," he said. "It is because although the Egyptians were cruel, they were still people. God did terrible things to them – and to show that we are sorry for their suffering, we don't drink to it. It shows that we treat everyone, even our worst enemies, as human beings."

Then the singing started. Elijah joined in all the songs. He even taught everyone some new songs as well. Debbie glowed with pride as she listened to Elijah singing in his splendid bass voice.

"Dad, you've forgotten something," cried Debbie. "We have to go and look for the afikoman!"

"So you do," agreed her dad. "Go on, take Ben and find it. We can't end Passover until you've got it. No one can go home, we're all trapped here."

Ben and Debbie searched everywhere.

"It's very small," groaned Ben. "It could be anywhere."

But then Ben found it under Debbie's pillow. When he came back holding it, everyone cheered.

"Give it to me," said Dad, holding out his hand, "and I'll give everyone a piece."

But Debbie knew that this was part of the game. "No, Ben, don't," she warned. "Make them give us chocolate first."

Solemnly Ben clung on to the afikoman and shook his head. "We'll swap it for four bars of chocolate each," he demanded.

"What crooks!" laughed Elijah. "These English children are bandits. But you'll have to meet their demands or we'll be here all night."

The children were munching contentedly on their chocolate when Elijah put his hand to his head. "Oh, no!" he cried. "We've forgotten something very important!"

"What?" demanded Debbie and Ben together.

"No one has opened the door to Elijah," said the old man.

"I did!" shouted Debbie.

"To me, yes – but maybe the Prophet wants to join us, too."

Debbie opened the front door again and looked outside. A draught blew in, but there was no Prophet Elijah.

"He didn't want to join us," said Debbie sadly.

"Did you really think he would?" asked her new friend gently.

"No, but I hoped."

"Now that is the whole point," continued the old man. "To carry on hoping, even when there is no encouragement – that is the real challenge."

"It's really hard," protested Debbie.

The old man looked into her eyes and smiled. "We've been waiting for him to come for thousands of years. And who knows, maybe he'll come next year."

"Maybe," said Debbie. "This has still been a wonderful Passover, Elijah. And it's all because of you!"

"Let's have a toast to Elijah," said Debbie's dad. "And this time we can all drink the wine." He turned to the old man and raised his glass. "To our new friend, Elijah. May he come next year and every year after."

Glossary

Afikoman A piece of matzah, (unleavened bread), hidden for children to find.

Charoset A delicious paste made from apple, cinnamon, almond and wine mixed together. The paste represents the cement that was used to build the pyramids, and its sweetness is a reminder of the sweetness of freedom.

Hagadah The book that tells the story of Passover. It is used as a guide for the ceremonies and songs.

Matzah (Matzot is the plural.) The flat biscuit-like bread that is eaten at Passover. The bread is made flat as a reminder of the time when the Jews had to leave Egypt so quickly that there wasn't even time to allow the yeast in the bread to rise.

Messiah The 'anointed one', who will come to Earth and make it a better place. Elijah is His prophet and will return first.

Pharaoh The king of Egypt, who enslaved the Jews.

Seder The traditional meal held on the first night of Passover.

Unleavened Bread that has not had time to rise and is flat and crisp. Matzah is unleavened bread.

CELEBRATION STORIES

Look out for these other titles in the **Celebration Stories** series:

A Present For Salima by Kerena Marchant
It's Ramadan, and Ibrahim is allowed to fast like the adults do
– as long as he drinks water during the day. So when he travels
to the mountains with his father, he stops at a small village for
a drink. Ibrahim is shocked to discover how hard it is for
Salima and the other villagers to get water. He realizes he has a
lot to be thankful for. He really wants to help – but how?

The Treasure of Santa Cruz by Saviour Pirotta
Salvador can't believe his luck. He's always wanted to carry the
cross of Santa Cruz in the Good Friday pageant and now he's
been chosen. It's a dream come true. But then tragedy strikes
and Salvador is asked to let his friend Juan take his place. How
can Salvador sacrifice something he's wanted for his whole life?

The Dragon Doorway by Clare Bevan
Nothing's going right for Nathan's family – Dad's broken his
big toe, the roof's leaking, and Mum's lost her pantomime job
as Goldy the Magic Chicken… So when a competition leaflet
comes through the door, promising a family ticket for a
mystery tour, Nathan thinks it's worth a try. All he's got to do is
solve a riddle. But no one seems to have a clue – until Nathan
finds the Dragon Doorway…

You can buy all these books from your local bookseller, or order them direct
from the publisher. For more information about **Celebration Stories,** write
to: *The Sales Department, Hodder Children's Books, a division of Hodder
Headline Limited, 338 Euston Road, London NW1 3BH.*